BiN Weevils .COM

THE OFFICIAL GUIDE
BiN-TASTIC UPDATED EDITION

First published 2011 by Macmillan Children's Books

This revised edition published 2013 by Macmillan Children's Books
a division of Macmillan Publishers Limited
20 New Wharf Road, London N1 9RR
Basingstoke and Oxford
Associated companies throughout the world
www.panmacmillan.com

ISBN 978-1-4472-3230-8

Written by William Petty and Bin Weevils Ltd

1 3 5 7 9 8 6 4 2

A CIP catalogue record for this book is available from the British Library.

Printed and bound in Italy by Printer Trento s.r.l.

CONTENTS

INTRODUCTION

Do you want to explore an amazing online world that's full of ever-changing fun? From the moment you create your unique Bin Weevil character, you'll be on a Bin-tastic journey filled with adventures, missions, challenges and games. Find your friends online and make tons of new buddies too as you meet all the wacky inhabitants of the Bin! Challenge your pals to games, solve fiendish puzzles and enter competitions to win brilliant prizes. Every day, you can explore a changing Binscape, unlock hidden secrets and put your wits to the test!

Together with your friends, you can watch the latest TV shows whenever you want, and even read extracts from cool new books. It won't be long before you're invited to incredible online parties, meeting the Bin's celebrities and picking up exclusive items for your Bin Nest. Your nest is your home within the Bin, which you can expand, decorate and customize to make it your very own. Shop for the perfect items, deck out your rooms and invite your buddies to come and check it out!

Your Bin Weevils adventure is waiting for you . . . so fall in and flip out!

This book will tell you everything you need to know about the Binscape.

With this book in hand, you'll be ready to explore and discover all the amazing things Bin Weevils has in store! You'll have the ultimate info right at your fingertips to make the most of your weevily experience.

Along the way you'll meet the characters, learn cool new secrets and pick up top tips to get ahead in the world of Bin Weevils! By the time you get to the end of the book, you'll be a certified Bin Weevils expert.

HIDDEN BAGS OF DOSH

Be on the lookout for the hidden Bags of Dosh throughout this book! Find them all and write down which pages you found them on – in order from the first page to the last. The numbers form a secret code that you can use to unlock a special nest item in the Mystery Code Machine in front of Lab's Lab!

The hidden Bags of Dosh look exactly like this. Count this one first, then find five more!

ITEM CODE:

7

_____   _____   _____   _____   _____   _____

Find the remaining Bags of Dosh to win a cool nest item!

Best moment:

Coming up with his latest and greatest plan!

TINK

If there's something crazy going on in the Bin, Tink's usually behind it! Never a day goes by without Tink coming up with a new harebrained scheme to earn Mulch. His plans almost always go wrong, but when you think you're a genius, you don't get put off easily – you think on your feet and come up with a new, equally loopy idea! With his best buddy Clott by his side, Tink is always happy to help the other residents of the Bin – whether they want him to or not!

Quote:

'I've got an idea!'

Greatest ambition:

To put on an amazing Bin Carnival!

CLOTT

Quote:
'That's brilliant, Tink!'

Clott is Tink's ever loyal, long-suffering best friend. These Boys from the Binscape are next-door neighbours, and they're always together, usually because Clott has been roped into another one of Tink's mad plans. Clott will do whatever he can to help out his friend, even when a more sensible Bin Weevil would have walked away. But that's what makes Clott such a useful partner – he doesn't do a lot of thinking! He's always trying to come up with ways to impress Posh, mostly with disastrous results.

Best moment:

Helping Tink in his mad plans.

POSH

Greatest ambition:
To impress Posh!

STAYING SAFE ONLINE

Follow these simple guidelines to help keep Bin Weevils a safe, friendly place to hang out!

• Never give out your real name. When you sign up to Bin Weevils, you will choose a unique Bin Weevil name – this is how other people on the site will know you, and you will be able to recognize your buddies by their Bin Weevil names.

• Never share your personal information. Don't tell other players where you live, how old you are, or where you go to school. You shouldn't ask others for this information either – don't ask anyone to tell you their real name, address, phone number, email address or password.

• Don't use bad language. Never swear or use words that other people might find offensive or unkind. Bullying and mean behaviour are not allowed!

• Don't put up with bad behaviour. If someone says something to upset you on the site, you can add them to your Ignore list, which means they won't be able to talk to you. Or you can report them to the site moderators, who will decide what to do.

• Play fair and don't cheat!

PASSWORD SAFETY

A good password is something that's easy for you to remember, but very hard for anyone else to guess! Never use your real name or any part of your Bin Weevil name as a password. It's a great idea to use a silly random word, or even a word you made up! Using a number in your password is another smart idea.

Never share passwords with anyone except a parent. If you share your password with someone else, they could log in to your account, spend all your Mulch and Dosh and turn your nest upside down! You wouldn't give anybody the key to your front door, so don't give other players your password.

Never ask your friends to share their password with you either – passwords are private!

If you think somebody else might know your password, change it as soon as you can by using the link underneath the login area.

NOW YOU'RE READY TO CREATE A BIN WEEVIL!
To do this, click on GET STARTED! on
the login page!

CONTROLS

Congratulations, you are now a Bin Weevil! Let's start off by having a look at the controls that let you interact with the Binscape!

LEVEL

This tells you what level your Bin Weevil has achieved, and how many Experience Points (or XP) you still need to reach the next level. The more you play, the higher your level goes, and the more cool items you'll be able to buy in the Shopping Mall! You'll also unlock new missions, special moves and activities as you level up.

MULCH

This is the Bin Weevils' currency, which can be spent on loads of cool items! You can earn Mulch by playing games, completing hunts, running your Bin Tycoon businesses and more!

DOSH

You can use Dosh coins to buy even more amazing weevily stuff! Spend these shiners to unlock new missions, buy hats or shop at Bin Mart and Nestco! Bin Tycoon members receive a salary of Dosh coins every month. Plus, you can earn extra coins from your BinCard!

FOOD

If your food bar is getting low, find a restaurant or a cafe and grab a snack!

EXPRESSIONS

Click this icon to pick an expression for your Bin Weevil's face. Let your friends know if you're feeling happy, sad, grumpy or even a bit silly!

BUDDY ALERTS

You can turn your live Buddy Alerts off and on. Buddy Alerts pop up to tell you when one of your Bin buddies has unlocked a new achievement or completed something fun in-game!

MAP

The map shows all the locations in the Bin and lets you get from place to place in the blink of an eye! You can always click on your nest in the bottom left corner of the map to get back home instantly.

TOP TIP
Play the Daily Brain Strain at Lab's Lab every day to earn lots of XP and Mulch.

MY STUFF BOX

This is where any items you find or buy will be stored. Click on it to see what's inside, then click on it again to close it.

ACTIONS MENU

Click here to see all the actions (special moves) that your Bin Weevil has unlocked so far. You can also use keys 1–5 for some moves.

MAKING FRIENDS

CHAT BAR
This is what you use to talk to other Bin Weevils. Type in what you want to say and press return or click on the 'send' button.

CHAT LOG
Click here to look back on recent conversations.

BUDDY LIST
This is a list of all your weevily friends. When another user asks to be your buddy, an envelope will pop up from here. Click on it to review your buddy invitations and accept new buddies.

IGNORE LIST
See a list of any Bin Weevils you have chosen to ignore.

NEST INVITATIONS
This is a list of all your invitations to visit other Bin Weevils' nests. Click on the envelope to see your list of invitations and pick which nest to go to first!

GUEST LIST
See and edit a list of the Bin Weevils you've invited to your nest!

MESSAGE INDICATOR
This symbol will let you know how many new buddy requests and nest invitations you have.

PROFILE BOX

Click on a Bin Weevil and their profile box will pop up.

 Send a buddy request to this Bin Weevil.

 Invite this Bin Weevil to your nest.

 Ignore this Bin Weevil (this means they can't talk to you).

 Report this Bin Weevil to a moderator.

If the Bin Weevil is already on your buddy list, the buttons will be slightly different:

 Find this buddy if they are online, or check when they last logged in if they are offline.

 Remove this buddy from your buddy list.

 Send a message to this buddy.

 If this buddy is currently on your ignore list, click here to take them off.

BUDDY LIST   BUDDY N

 Bunty

 Clott

 Dosh

 Flam

 Lab

 Posh

 Tink

SPECIAL TYCOON CONTROLS!

Go straight to Tycoon TV Towers.

Take a picture of you and your friends at any time!

TOP TIP
Buddies who are online right now in the same Bin as you will appear in dark letters.

 15

BECOME A BIN TYCOON

Become a Bin Tycoon member to have the MOST weevily fun and get loads of exclusive Tycoon rewards!

Expand your Bin Garden - Plant more cool stuff in a bigger area!

Earn a monthly salary of Dosh - Get more Dosh to spend every month on nest items, missions and hats!

WELCOME TYCOON ISLAND

Get VIP treatment at parties – You'll have access to exclusive prizes, games and party rooms!

Own your own businesses – Open your own Tycoon Plaza for business, and fit out glittering nightclubs and a chic photographic studio.

Create your own magazine – You're the editor-in-chief, and you decide what the whole Bin simply has to know about!

Get bonus rewards from your BinCard – Collect rare seeds, shopping vouchers, extra puzzle pieces and other goodies!

WELCOME TO YOUR NEST

TOP TIP
Agent Clott holds the secret to finding the Secret Weevil Service.

GARDEN

GARDEN PIPE Click here to step outside into your Bin Garden. Turn to page 26 to find out more about gardens!

BIN BOTS
Click on this mysterious door to enter the world of the Bin Bots!

NEST ROOMS
Each Bin Weevil starts with one room, so only one door will be open. But that can all change as you start expanding your nest to unlock up to ten rooms!

MAILBOX
If you get sent a direct message by one of your buddies, it will show up in here. Your mailbox will flash to let you know you've got mail!

TYCOON FAIR UPDATE!

Scribbles' nest
NEST COOLNESS: 2053

COLOUR SLIDER
Adjust the colour in your nest's entrance hall!

NEST COOLNESS Your Nest Coolness changes when you redecorate your nest, and goes up when other Bin Weevils give your nest a good rating! To learn more, turn to page 23!

NEST NEWS
If there's a party coming up, a hot new competition or exciting changes to the Bin Weevils' world, you can guarantee the story will be here first!

BINCARD
Earn daily prizes with your BinCard! Turn the page to learn more.

Bin Tycoon!

How do I get another room for my nest?
To buy a new nest room, visit Rigg's Property Shop on the top floor of the Shopping Mall!

FUEL-O-METER
The more stuff you have in your nest, the more fuel you need to keep your lights on and your gadgets powered up. Click on the Fuel-o-Meter to keep your fuel topped up regularly, or you could find your nest plunged into darkness – and what sort of impression is that going to make on your guests?

Click on the stamp to mark your card and claim your daily BinCard Reward!

Click on these buttons to view your Vouchers and Puzzle Pieces . . . once you have earned some!

BinCard

BinCard every day to earn all your rewards! Each time you stamp... ...next prize. To collect all the rewards, you'll need to be a B... ...ber:

MY VOUCHERS

M... ...ZZLES

BinCard #1 - TINK

Click on any upcoming reward space to find out more about the reward and see what treats are in store for you!

Rewards with a top-hat icon can only be earned by Tycoons. To collect every exclusive reward, become a Bin Tycoon member!

Scribbles' nest

NEST COOLNESS: 205

When you log in, click the icon on your nest wall to view your BinCard.

MORE STAMPS = MORE COOL REWARDS!

Exclusive seeds for your garden!

Vouchers for discounts on hats, missions, items and more!

Free Dosh coins to spend on anything!

Puzzle pieces to collect – finish a puzzle and win a secret prize item!

Free Mulch to buy whatever you like!

Free XP to help you level up faster!

DECORATE YOUR NEST

The MY STUFF box holds all your nest items. Whenever you buy an item from a shop, claim a prize from a party, collect a fan poster or earn a trophy, all your stuff will appear in here.

DECORATING

To place an item in your nest, click on the treasure-chest icon to open the MY STUFF box, then click and drag the items you want into your nest room. You will have to open up the MY STUFF box whenever you want to move items around inside your nest rooms or move items in and out of your nest.

ROOM RATING

Whenever you invite someone to visit your nest, they can rate your rooms! Good ratings will earn you more XP and will help to raise your Nest Coolness. Impress your guests with a stunning nest!

ORNAMENTS

Some items, like trophies, can only be placed on shelves and tabletops, so you will need to buy some before you can show off your awards!

TOP TIP

To find items that go well together use the theme tags on the right side when you shop at Bin Mart or Nestco!

The MY STUFF box only shows you items that can be placed in the room in which you're standing. If you've bought items for a business or seeds for your garden, you will need to move to the correct location before you'll see those items in your box.

23

BEST NESTS

With the right combination of items and accessories, you can build a brilliant nest room! You can even win a Bin Nest Trophy if your design impresses the Nest Inspector. To learn more about the Nest Inspector and to read some cool tips on decorating your nest, see page 36.

Turn your nest into a toy workshop . . . .

. . . Or go back to medieval times!

Living in luxury!

YOUR BIN GARDEN

Planting and harvesting your Bin Garden is loads of fun! Purchase some seeds from the Garden Shop, plant them in your garden and watch them grow into zany, wacky and wonderful flowers, mushrooms, trees and more! When they're ready, you can harvest them to earn your reward.

Some plants will wither and die after a certain time, so make sure you check on them regularly and harvest them while you can. Other plants remain in your garden forever and can be harvested over and over again. Permanent plants and statues can be moved around your garden to give it a brand-new look.

To buy a watering can, and more seeds, you'll need to visit the Garden Shop. It's in the Shopping Mall, but there's a shortcut to get there from your garden – just click on the sign that says BUY SEEDS.

BUY SEEDS

To water a plant, first place your watering can anywhere in your garden. Then click on the plant you want to care for. If the plant can be watered, you will see WATER as an option in its mini menu.

TOP TIP

If a plant looks a little sad and dull, it needs to be watered.

CLICK . . . IF YOU DARE! Clicking on a plant will tell you how close it is to being fully grown or ready to harvest. But some plants also animate when you click. Yeow! This Venus Flytrap is vicious!

TOP TIP

Place your biggest and tallest items (giant beanstalks, trees, statues etc.) at the back of your garden, and your smaller plants, flowers and mushrooms at the front. This way, you'll be able to see everything and you won't miss harvesting any plants that are hidden behind others!

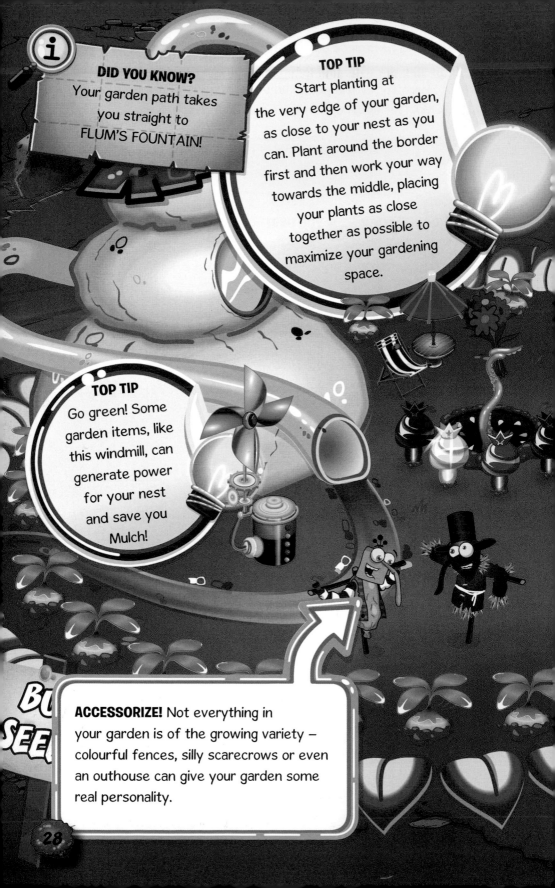

TOP TIP
Start planting at the very edge of your garden, as close to your nest as you can. Plant around the border first and then work your way towards the middle, placing your plants as close together as possible to maximize your gardening space.

TOP TIP
Go green! Some garden items, like this windmill, can generate power for your nest and save you Mulch!

ACCESSORIZE! Not everything in your garden is of the growing variety – colourful fences, silly scarecrows or even an outhouse can give your garden some real personality.

BU
SEE

28

THE GARDEN INSPECTOR

Quote:

'Go green!'

The Garden Inspector loves being surrounded by greenery. She is seldom found indoors, and prefers to spend most of her time hopping from garden to garden, awarding trophies for the best ones she sees. The Garden Inspector firmly believes that plants need music to thrive, so she sings opera to them at every opportunity. She's been known to sleep outside in her lawn chair so the plants don't get lonely at night!

Best moment: Discovering the magical powers of the Giant Beanstalk seed.

Greatest ambition:
To collect one of every rare seed.

This is your Bin Nest. Click here whenever you want to return home.

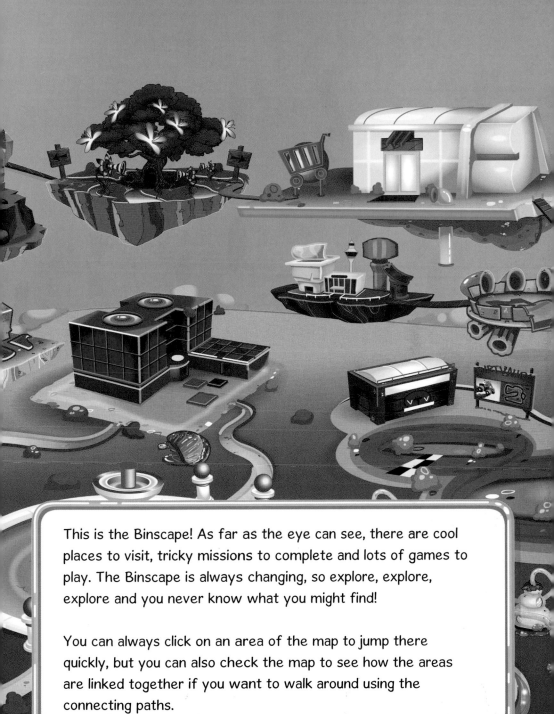

This is the Binscape! As far as the eye can see, there are cool places to visit, tricky missions to complete and lots of games to play. The Binscape is always changing, so explore, explore, explore and you never know what you might find!

You can always click on an area of the map to jump there quickly, but you can also check the map to see how the areas are linked together if you want to walk around using the connecting paths.

DOSH'S PALACE

MULCH SHOOT

PLAY GAME

Dosh's Palace is elegant and sophisticated in every way. Magnificent fish-head fountains spew forth delightful torrents of dirty water either side of its imposing facade. This place just oozes luxury!

TOP SECRET

Click on all the rubies on the side of Dosh's Palace and prepare to be amazed!

DOSH

Quote:
'There's nothing like squeaky-clean Mulch . . . except nice shiny Dosh coins!'

Dosh is the richest Bin Weevil – he's absolutely rolling in Mulch! He's so incredibly, Bin-tastically rich that he even invented his own currency, the Dosh coin. When Dosh isn't busy spending all his lovely loot, he's cleaning it. He loves nothing more than to put his Mulch notes through the wash and polish his stacks of Dosh coins until they sparkle!

Best moment:
Opening the brand-new Bank on Tycoon Island!

Greatest ambition:
To build the tallest stack of Mulch ever recorded.

THE BIN WEEVIL CHANGER

Inside Dosh's Palace, you'll find the amazing Bin Weevil Changer machine. Here you can choose the shape and colour of your Bin Weevil's head, eyes, body, legs and antennae. When you find a look you're happy with, save it and exit!

Any time you're bored with your look, you can pop back into Dosh's Palace and give your Bin Weevil a full makeover! From the shape of your body to the colour of your antennae, for just a small amount of Mulch you can give your Bin Weevil a whole new style.

DID YOU KNOW?
The Bin Weevil Changer was built by Dosh's Great-Uncle Slosh, a brilliant but mad inventor!

CHANGE THE WAY YOUR BIN WEEVIL LOOKS HERE!

BIN WEEVIL CHANGER ⓘ

DID YOU KNOW?
There are over six billion possible combinations, so you'll never run out of unique Bin Weevil looks to try out!

If you're very lucky, you might get a special gift from Dosh himself! Generous Dosh has been known to shower free Mulch down on the grateful Bin Weevils below, so get your clicking fingers ready in case you see some Mulch raining from the balcony!

TOP TIP
Want to attract attention and draw a crowd? Visit Dosh's Palace with some buddies and change your colours to match each other! Everyone will stop and stare when they see a big group of lime-green Bin Weevils hanging out at Flum's Fountain!

35

Quote:
'It's absolutely fabulous!'

THE NEST INSPECTOR

The Nest Inspector is a very special Bin Weevil. His job is to discover the very best nests around! When he finds a nest that is absolutely Bin-tastic, he awards the owner an exclusive Bin Nest Trophy either in bronze, silver or gold. These trophies are not sold in shops – the only way to get your weevily fingers on one of them is to impress the Nest Inspector with a stunning pad! The Nest Inspector loves his job, but he also loves his holidays, and can often be found sipping on a cold smoothie at the beach.

Best moment: Discovering a trophy-winning nest!

Greatest ambition: To design the bestselling nest item of all time.

HOW DO I GET A BIN NEST TROPHY?

If your Nest Coolness is high enough, you'll be able to snap and submit pictures of your fabulous nest for the Nest Inspector's approval! If your nest knocks his six socks off, you might find a glimmering trophy waiting for you!

The Nest Inspector also has his very own magazine, BEST NEST. The mag is packed full of inspiring images of the coolest nests he's recently visited! You can find BEST NEST inside Weevil Post at Rigg's Multiplex.

TOP TIP
To get your Nest Coolness up, make sure you decorate all your rooms and invite lots of buddies over to rate them!

NEST CHECKLIST

All rooms fully decorated! ✔   Fill up your shelves! ✔

Themed rooms are fab! ✔   Don't forget the flooring! ✔

Lighting brightens things up! ✔   Collections are cool! ✔

THE SHOPPING MALL

If you've got some Mulch and Dosh burning a hole in your pocket, visit the Shopping Mall for some retail therapy. Everything you could possibly want is on sale here, from brilliant themed wallpaper to insane gadgets and golden toilets!

BIN-MART

DID YOU KNOW? If an item is marked LOW STOCK, there aren't very many of them left. Snap up this item while you still can! When an item goes out of stock, it won't be available until the shopkeeper orders some more.

MEET THE BIN WEEVILS

FLEM

Flem has a perpetual cold, and when he doesn't have a cold, he has hay fever! Sniffle, snort, snuffle, sniff, that's how you know when Flem's around. Still, he doesn't let the sniffles get him down. He keeps himself busy rearranging his furniture and recommending the very best new nest items. That, and getting through a whole lorry-load of tissues!

Quote:

'SNIFFFF!'

Best moment:

The time he went a whole hour without sneezing.

Greatest ambition:

To expand his manor and overtake Dosh's Palace in luxury.

40

FURNITURE

Nom, nom! Comfy AND delicious!

Set sail for the high seas!

Take a seat in royal style!

MEET THE BIN WEEVILS

ZING

Quote:

'Zowie!'

Greatest ambition:

To memorize every word that begins with the letter Z.

Zing is a zany Bin Weevil who's always zooming around with zest. She absolutely can't stay still for more than an instant, which is why her favourite gadgets are the ones that never stop moving! From robots to rocket ships, Zing knows everything there is to know about gadgets and gizmos! The only thing she loves more than gadgets is the letter Z.

Best moment: Seeing Lab's top-secret super-laser plans!

GADGETS & GIZMOS

Wonder what's inside your Bin Weevil?

Keep your nest items under watch!

Kit out your own mad-science lab!

GRUNT

Quote:

[a series of excitable grunting sounds]

Grunt is a true plumbing enthusiast. He's won the Golden Plunger Award for Bin Weevils' Services to Toilets every year for as long as anyone can remember – although he may well be the only one who enters!

Although Grunt rarely speaks, his knowledge of tubs, toilets, sinks and tiles cannot be matched. His favourite nest item of all time is the Golden Toilet. So if your toilet ever needs repairing, Grunt's your Bin Weevil!

Best moment:

Winning the Golden Plunger Award of course!

Greatest ambition:

To rework all the leaky plumbing in Gam's Castle!

MEET THE BIN WEEVILS

FAB

Greatest ambition: To cheer everyone up!

Fab loves everything and everyone – you won't find a nicer Bin Weevil anywhere in the Binscape. Everything in Fab's world is sunshine and rainbows and butterflies and . . . well, it's just fab! She loves flicking through BEST NEST magazine to see all the beautiful floors, walls and ceilings. Fab's seen it all when it comes to interior decorating, but when she visited Clott's place, imagine her surprise to find that he had wallpapered the ceiling and installed a window on the floor!

Quote:

'What a beautiful Bin day – isn't it fab?'

Best moment: Designing a custom-made carpet for Dosh's Palace.

46

FLOORS, WALLS & CEILINGS

Pick 'n' mix on your walls!

Add an eye-popping rug!

Run out on to the pitch!

MEET THE BIN WEEVILS

TAB

If there was a world championship in worrying, Tab would take gold, silver and bronze. He worries from the moment he wakes up in the morning until the moment he falls asleep (which sometimes isn't until he's spent the whole night lying awake worrying). When Bin Weevils come into his shop, he worries. When no Bin Weevils come into his shop, he worries! Basically, Tab worries a lot.

Best moment:

When he's asleep!

Quote:
'Be careful!'

Greatest ambition:

To have nothing to worry about apart from the fact that he has nothing to worry about!

48

THE GARDEN SHOP

Sometimes wishes really do come true . . .

It goes down in flames and comes back more beautiful!

The shining jewel in any Bin Tycoon's garden!

RIGG

Quote:

'I built that!' (Even when he didn't!)

Best moment:

When he sacked Tink and Clott.

Rigg is a big character in the Binscape. He thinks big, he acts big, he's got a big head and a big heart. He's also into building big buildings – his construction projects are everywhere, and he's always got a plan for what to build next. Sometimes his big imagination makes him say he built something even when he didn't, but nobody minds. He once hired Tink and Clott to work on his building site. That was a BIG mistake!

Greatest ambition:

To build a suspension bridge to Mulch Island.

RIGG'S PROPERTY SHOP

At Rigg's Property Shop you can expand your nest by purchasing extra nest rooms! If you're running out of space to display all those cool nest items, trophies and posters, it's time to branch out and invest in some weevily real estate! Remember, the more rooms you have, the faster your nest coolness and XP will accumulate! You can find Rigg's Property Shop on the top floor of the Shopping Mall.

To buy more space for your nest, choose a room from the floor plans.

NEST FLOOR PLANS

BUY YOUR BUSINESS PLAZA HERE!

Purchase a Bin Tycoon Plaza here!

51

BIN PETS

Bin Pets are loads of fun, and training them is an exciting challenge! If you're ready to adopt a pet, you can find the Bin Pet Shop in the Shopping Mall.

The first thing to do when you get your pet back to your nest is to place its bowl and basket in one of the rooms.

Your pet lives in your nest – whenever you log out of Bin Weevils, your pet will climb into the basket and go to sleep. It will be waiting for you when you return, eager to play!

XP: Learning and performing tricks increases your pet's XP.

Energy: Moving around and doing tricks will tire out your pet so its energy bar will go down. If your pet's energy is low, it needs to rest.

Food: This bar goes down when your pet is hungry. If it gets to red, your pet needs food urgently! Try to feed your pet when the bar is orange.

Health: If your pet has had too much or too little to eat, or gets unfit or tired, its health bar will go down. But some good care will bring it back to good health quickly!

Fitness: Doing lots of actions will make your pet fitter.

Orange

XP: 10856

ENERGY
FOOD
HEALTH
FITNESS

DON'T PANIC!

If you can't remember what to do, don't worry. This button on your pet profile will take you straight to the Bin Pet Guide!

TOP TIP

Reward your pet when it learns something new. Hold the mouse over your pet for a few seconds to give it a stroke – this will make it learn faster.

PET TRAINING

There are three types of skills your pet can learn:

General skills
Your pet learns to listen to commands such as 'stay' and 'sit'.

Orange

XP: 10356

ENERGY
FOOD
HEALTH
FITNESS

Ball skills
Pets can be trained to fetch and throw balls, or even juggle!

Spinning skills
Your pet can perform a variety of acrobatic twists and spins.

It's important to keep your pet happy and healthy — it will tell you if something is wrong. If your pet starts to get tired, it will need to go to bed and rest. Don't wake it up until its energy levels have gone up, or it will just go back to sleep again.

When your pet gets hungry, click on the bowl to give it some food. Make sure you don't overfeed it though — your pet will eat whatever you give it, and too much food is unhealthy! Pet food can also be purchased at the Bin Pet Shop.

DID YOU KNOW?
Bin Pets like to play with other Bin Pets! Try taking your pet outside for a walk and see how it acts when it meets another Bin Pet.

TOP TIP
Having trouble getting your Bin Pet to jump on your back? Before asking your pet to 'jump on', make sure you are standing right next to it or it will not be able to reach you.

CLUB FLING

Fling's a Bin Weevil who just can't stop dancing! Fling couldn't understand why nightclubs are only open at night, so he decided to open his own club, which is open 24/7! No matter the time of day or night, if you're in the mood for dancing you'll find the disco ball glittering at Fling's!

DID YOU KNOW? Bin Tycoons can work together to unleash some extra XP! Three Bin Weevils will need to stand on the three white lights over the entrance. Stay put, and watch the tube opposite fill with a strange purple goo. When the goo reaches the top, it'll explode in a shower of bubbles, filling the air with valuable XP to collect! Click on it quickly before it disappears!

It's all happening here at the coolest club in the Binscape! Outside, see if you can get the party started with some giant party blowers. Then step inside to show off your funkiest moves on the dance floor, before spinning some tunes on the decks.

Bin Tycoons can head upstairs to the chill-out zone and relax on the comfy cushions, grab a snack or play a game with friends. Outside on the roof are more ace games to play, and the Bin's biggest confetti cannon!

SLAM'S PARTY BOX
For even more weevily party action, dance your way over to Slam's Party Box! You never know what adventures await you at the Binscape's other hot party spot!

INSIDE CLUB FLING

The dance floor inside Club Fling is a great place to show off your weevily moves. Doing special moves is fun when you're hanging out with buddies! Can you spin at the same time?

DID YOU KNOW?
Clicking on the buttons beside the DJ booth will activate some awesome strobe light effects – perfect if you're taking a pic!

MEET THE BIN WEEVILS

FLING

Fling's got dancing fever, and he's got it bad! He likes his music loud and his feet moving. Most Bin Weevils can't work out what Fling's on about half the time, but luckily his funky moves speak for themselves. He's strutted his stuff all over the Bin, and he makes sure the hottest tunes are spinning at Club Fling, the Bin's must-visit dance spot.

Best moment: Winning the Bin Weevils dance-off.

Greatest ambition: To always win the Bin Weevils dance-off!

KONNECT MULCH

Aim: To make a line of four of your colour Mulch Balls.

How to play: Take turns with your opponent to drop a Mulch Ball into the rack. It will fall all the way to the bottom. Use your Mulch to make a line of four, while trying to stop your opponent from getting four in a row.

TOP TIP

If you go first, drop your Mulch in the middle column – it will give you the best chance of winning!

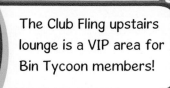

The Club Fling upstairs lounge is a VIP area for Bin Tycoon members!

TOP TIP

If you get your Mulch in one of the four corner squares, it's there to stay – your opponent won't be able to flip it back again.

FLIP MULCH

Aim: To end up with more of your colour Mulch on the board than your opponent.

How to play: Take turns putting a Mulch Ball on the board. Every time you make a line of Mulch with your colour at each end and your opponent's colour in the middle, all their Mulch flips over and becomes YOUR Mulch! But watch out – it could all flip back again next go!

TOP SECRET Jump on all the cushions in Fling's Lounge to discover a silly surprise!

61

THE POOL HALL

A world away from the glitz of Club Fling, the Pool Hall is where down-to-earth Bin Weevils like to come for a game of pool in gritty, grungy surroundings. The floor may be dirty, and the wallpaper may be peeling, but it feels like home!

Aim: To pot all your opponent's balls before they can pot yours.

How to play: To hit one of your balls, click on it, drag back, and release. Choose the angle and power of each shot to knock the other player's balls into the pockets.

TOP TIP
If your balls end up near the edges of the table and far from the pockets, they will be harder to pot.

TOP TIP

Practise potting your opponent's ball with your very first shot – if you can master this, you'll be unstoppable!

63

FLUM'S FOUNTAIN

Flum's Fountain is an awesome place to chat with buddies and get to know new Bin Weevils – it's where everyone stops to chill, and there's a reason it's named after the Bin's most famous reporter!

You can water the mushrooms to make them grow! To do this, you'll need to make the fountain spray jets of water in their direction.

To set off a jet of water, jump on the lit-up blue pads that activate randomly around the border of the fountain. Act quickly to jump on to a pad while it's still lit up!

TOP TIP

If you've interviewed somebody for your mag, ask them to join you at Flum's Fountain for a pic. Zoom right in on them to get the perfect front-cover snap!

64

FREE CAM

While you're hanging out with your pals, try using the Free Cam to look at the world in a different way. Not only can you get a clearer view of the growing mushrooms, but you can also move the camera in close to see your own Bin Weevil or a buddy in more detail. Wow!

By clicking the different buttons and sliders on the Free Cam, you can look around 360 degrees. Use the zoom slider if you want to take a closer peek at something.

MULCH	EXPERIENCE

Growing these mushrooms will earn you these bonuses!

 2 XP

 5 Mulch

 5 XP

 10 Mulch

 10 XP

 20 Mulch

 20 XP

 75 Mulch

 15 XP

50 Mulch

 100 Mulch

 50 XP

 500 Mulch

Work together to collect them all!

It's always showtime at Rigg's place! The Multiplex is Rigg's pride and joy, his greatest achievement to date. There were some memorable moments while it was being built, many of them not so pleasant for Rigg . . . Whenever Tink and Clott are involved, there are bound to be a few disasters! However, the structure finally went up and this famous Bin cinema is now a haven for celebrities and cool Bin Weevils alike. It's a great place to watch top shows from the best kids' TV networks. You can even catch up on the madcap antics of Tink and Clott in the Bin Weevils cartoons!

CASH MACHINE

You can find plenty of cash machines, just like this one, dotted around the Binscape! Bin Tycoons can collect their monthly Dosh salary here, as well as rake in all the Mulch earnings from their businesses!

DID YOU KNOW? You can read magazines written by other Bin Weevils by clicking on the news stand. A random selection of mags will be listed each time. If you want to read a specific Bin Weevil's mag, click on him or her and select the magazine icon from their profile box.

FIGG'S CAFE

If your tummy is rumbling, head to Figg's Cafe for some yummy grub. There's always something delicious on the menu to fill you up. Or why not help out by serving food to hungry Bin Weevils? They're sure to thank you!

Several famous Bin Weevils have dined at Figg's Cafe today, but each one of them has forgetfully left something behind! Look at the lost items for clues and help Figg unjumble the famous names.

The answers are on page 158.

MENU

TLTCO

BESISLRBC

HODS

GLNFI

SETN PCRTNIEOS

69

WEEVIL POST

Step in here to grab your copy of BEST NEST or WEEVIL WEEKLY, two of the Bin's most popular mags!

Could you use a bit of extra Mulch? Of course you could! So don't forget to swing by one of the three Mulch-Tastic Kiosks and pick up your daily free ticket! Create your own personalized ticket by scrolling through the symbols until you reckon you've found a lucky combination.

Every three days at 5 p.m., a lucky ticket will be picked, and if any of its symbols are in the same place as on your ticket, you're a Mulch winner! The more symbols that match the winning ticket, the more you'll get. Don't worry if your symbols don't come up – you can choose a new ticket every day.

TOP TIP
The Mulch draw happens every three days, but you can get four tickets for each draw if you're clever! Claim your first ticket on the day of the draw, right after the draw is finished. Then claim one on the next two days, and on the third day – the day of the next draw – pick one up before the draw takes place!

71

DIRT VALLEY

If you like to race, this is your place!
Prove you've got the sharpest driving
skills in the Bin as you take on one,
two or three other Bin Weevils
in thrilling races. There are three
awesome 3D tracks to master, all
with different difficulty levels.

In-game action

GAME CONTROLS

fire active
weapon

↑

steer
left

steer
right

← ↓ →

brake

Z
accelerate

X
turbo

Before you race against others, do a few practice laps in the time trials. When you think you're ready, pick a car and wait for some challengers. You'll need to win a trophy on each track before you can move on to the next one. If you're the day's top racer, you'll even get to see your name in lights over the track — and so will everyone else!

TOP TIP
You can use the turbo button (X) all the time, but be sure to release it when you need to get more grip on the corners.

BUBBLES - As you zoom around the track, pick up all the bubbles you can along the way to get cool items that you can use to slow down your competitors.

SLIME PAT - Drop this oily mess in front of another racer and they'll spin out! But be careful — you might hit it yourself on the next lap.

HOMING SPLAT - Beware of any racer with this yellow cloud above them. Don't get too close or it will home in on you!

STINK SHOT - Use this if you want to hit the racer in front of you.

TRACK 1

TRACK 2

TRACK 3

Hi, I'm Zip! I'm one of the fastest Bin Weevils on four wheels – even if Ham doesn't like to admit it! Here you can help me test and rate some of the newest tracks. To earn a place as a Track Tester you'll need to be a really speedy racer.

TOP TIP
A track that's interesting is more likely to earn you a good rating. Add some adventure to your track by customizing it with carefully placed obstacles and jump ramps!

SELECT A TRACK

Ham's the name and racing's the game! You won't find a speedier dirt-devil than me! Select a wicked track to race on from the menu over here and see if you can beat your buddies' top times.

TRACK BUILDER

Design, assemble and test your very own custom racetrack here! Once it's ready, our trusty Track Testers will have a go. If they think your track's a winner, it'll soon be available for everyone to race on. Plus, every time someone completes three laps of your track, you'll earn some bonus Mulch!

LAB'S LAB

The roof of Lab's Lab is bristling with sciency stuff for finding out about the world. Lab's Lab is the home of all that is brainy and mind-boggling in the Bin, and this is the place to come for the Daily Brain Strain.

TOP SECRET

Lab loves Crazy Eights! Click the 8-Ball on the top of Lab's Lab eight times to see one of Lab's tricks!

STERY CODE MACHINE

GENERATE

HAVE YOU GOT A SECRET ITEM CODE TO REDEEM?

In front of Lab's Lab sits a mysterious machine that contains ultra-exclusive secret nest items. If you've found a secret Bin Weevils item code, you can enter it here to unlock your item. Hint: You can find some secret codes hiding right here in this book!

LAB

Quote:

'I know the answer to that!'

Lab is the Bin's very own mad scientist. Well, he's not THAT mad compared to some of the other characters wandering the Binscape . . . but he sure is mad about knowing stuff! This brainbox knows nearly everything, which is why he can breeze through the Brain Strain without his bulging brain even breaking a sweat. He's full of fantastic facts that he's happy to share with the other Bin Weevils. He's also fascinated by Clott, because Clott looks at the world in a totally different way from anyone else. Well, he's sure got that right!

Greatest ambition:

To know everything backwards.

Best moment: Unveiling his maddest creation at the Mad Scientist Party.

DAILY BRAIN STRAIN

Warm up for the Brain Strain with these practice questions. It's a race, so time how long you take to answer them (see page 158)!

How many squares?

How many circles?

Time's Up!

A.M.

Digital time: __:__

P.M.

Digital time: __:__

Flag Test!

| Norway | China |
| Japan | Portugal |

4 x ? = 16

- 3
- 4
- 5
- 6

23 − 9 = ?

- 16
- 13
- 14
- 8

 79

FLEM MANOR

There's always lots of creative stuff going on at Flem Manor – it's delightfully arty! Before you pop inside to soak up some weevily culture, make sure you have a crack at the Spot the Difference puzzles in the tent outside – wow, are they tough!

Spot the Difference

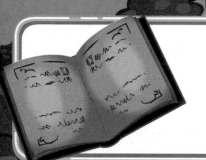

Once inside Flem Manor, sweep majestically up the grand staircase and hang a right to the library, where you can check out extracts from the coolest new books.

Spot

Flem Manor is also the place to be for word puzzles! Take a wander into the crossword and wordsearch room if you're low on Mulch. Each puzzle you complete will earn you a nice reward.

BTINKLSO
UPNSDDJK
NMKIPAOT
TUMRNETC
YCLOTTHY

Photo 1

SPOT THE DIFFERENCE!

Photo 2

Can you spot the ten differences?

81

WORD PUZZLES

Complete the puzzles to test your word skills!

The wordsearch words can be found horizontally, vertically and diagonally.

The answers are on page 159.

```
K N E S M U L T I P L A Y E R
P M I R T A A T Y C O O N D W
X D I G D U G N F L E V E L Q
B C E S H O D A T S G A M E S
E I H C S T S I Z E Z C T S C
B X N A O I C H O I N D A E O
X B P S L R O L Y F N N Q C M
J C M E C L A N U O H E A R P
B P R Y R A E T S B A R H E E
C U A O S I P N E D R A A T T
B H D R W T E E G K V C T S I
J O A D T N E N B E E I S H T
H U N T I Y J R C G S N L O I
F O O D Y E Z U Y E T G O P O
E I T E M S S Y N M U L C H N
```

ANTENNAE	DOSH	LEVEL	RACING
BINSCAPE	EXPERIENCE	MAGAZINE	SECRETS
BUDDIES	FOOD	MISSIONS	SHOP
CHALLENGE	GAMES	MULCH	STUDIO
CHAT	HARVEST	MULTIPLAYER	TYCOON
COMPETITION	HATS	MYSTERY	
CROWN	HUNT	NIGHTCLUB	
DECORATE	ITEMS	PARTY	

ACROSS

3. Tink's best Bin buddy
5. This intrepid reporter is editor-in-chief of WEEVIL WEEKLY
6. You can make this drink in a game on Tycoon Island
8. You'll find the Bin's racetrack at Dirt _ _ _ _ _ _
9. This Bin Weevil loves to dance!
11. To get to Mulch Island, you'll have to catch a plane at Rum's _ _ _ _ _ _ _ _
14. Collect a seed at Tink's Tree and plant it in your _ _ _ _ _ _ _
15. This Bin Weevil is always sniffling!
16. If you impress the Nest Inspector, he might give you this
17. If your nest has gone dark, you'll have to buy more of this
18. This Bin Weevil sells hats on Tycoon Island

DOWN

1. Go to Rigg's Property Shop to buy more _ _ _ _ _ _ for your nest!
2. Bin Pets like to juggle with these
4. To enter a competition, you need to visit Gong's _ _ _ _ _ _ _ _ _
7. This Bin Weevil owns the cafe next to Rigg's Movie Multiplex
10. The oldest Bin Weevil in the Bin
12. To change your Bin Weevil's look, you will have to enter Dosh's _ _ _ _ _ _
13. The best Bin Burger is served at Tum's _ _ _ _ _ _
15. Scribbles got his nickname because he loves to write, but his name is actually _ _ _ _ _

THE EDITOR'S OFFICE

Bin Tycoons who want to publish their own magazines flock to Flem Manor to get their fingers inky. To the right of the hall, at the bottom of the stairs, you'll find the Editor's Office. Once you're inside, just click on the editor's desk to get started!

SCRIBBLES' ADVICE:

1. Interviews are loads of fun to read! Hanging around in a social area like Flum's Fountain (my personal favourite) is a great place to find fascinating Bin Weevils to interview for your mag.

2. A picture always makes your story more interesting! When there's a new party or a new area in the Bin, weevil on over with your camera in tow to snap that perfect shot!

3. The more players who read and rate your mag, the more Mulch you'll earn! Other Bin Weevils can read your mag by clicking on you, so be online at busy times and mention your new mag to everyone you meet. If they've got a mag too, be sure to read and rate theirs in return!

MEET THE BIN WEEVILS

SCRIBBLES

Quote:

'That's interesting . . . tell me more!'

Scribbles's real name is Flum, but everyone knows him by his nickname. He's always been called Scribbles because he's seldom without a pen in his hand and he's always scribbling things down! He's the editor-in-chief of the popular WEEVIL WEEKLY magazine, and he's never happier than when he's roaming the Binscape, intrepidly chasing down an exclusive story to bring to his readers. If you see this roving reporter out and about, don't miss the opportunity to talk to him — he could make your name famous if he interviews you for his mag!

Best moment:

The publication of the first issue of WEEVIL WEEKLY magazine.

Greatest ambition:

To interview every Bin Weevil in the Bin.

INTERVIEW WITH SCRIBBLES

Scribbles is always on the move, interviewing Bin Weevils all over the Bin. But this time the tables are turned! We asked what YOU wanted to know about our favourite reporter, and you sent in your questions for Scribbles! Here are some of his answers.

carly57 -
What's your favourite place in the Bin?

You might think it's Flum's Fountain because it was named after me. But my favourite place is actually the Editor's Office inside Flem Manor, because that's where my WEEVIL WEEKLY magazine comes to life!

froggy2003 -
Where do you get all of your brilliant ideas from?

My fans, of course! I like to interview Bin Weevils and ask lots of questions.

reyi -
Scribbles, what does Bin Weevils mean to you?

Bin Weevils means everything to me! Without the Bin and my weevily fans, I would be lost!

27club –
Do you think all Bin Weevils are equal no matter what their experience and level?

Absolutely YES! You should only judge a Bin Weevil by their personality.

Winniem –
What first gave you the idea to make WEEVIL WEEKLY?

A long time ago I noticed that many Bin Weevils had a lot of great questions, opinions and ideas. I thought about how I could share what I saw and heard with every Bin Weevil. What better way to do this than to start up a weekly magazine!

tashatoucan –
What's your favourite crazy move?

I love to do several moves at the same time: jump, head shake and arms swinging in the air! Are you wondering how it is possible to do all three moves at once? It's simple – just try pressing the numbers 1, 2, 3, 4 on your keyboard really fast!

x-PurpleAngel-x -
Why do you like writing magazines?

My favourite thing of all time is writing WEEVIL WEEKLY magazine! I love being a reporter because you get to play detective and try to dig up interesting stories. When something happens in the Binscape I also like to interview and hear other Bin Weevils' opinions. Being a reporter allows me to meet interesting Bin Weevils every day – that's why I love it so much!

princess-cutie1 -
What is your favourite game in the Bin?

My favourite game is the Brain Strain puzzles at Lab's Lab. I think Lab did a great job in designing them. He is super-smart and I like that about him!

cali37 -
How do you feel with all the attention?

I like the attention. But sometimes there are lots of Bin Weevils talking to me and I can't talk to everyone at once. My biggest worry is coming across as rude! I try my weevily best to talk to as many Bin Weevils as possible.

CASTLE GAM

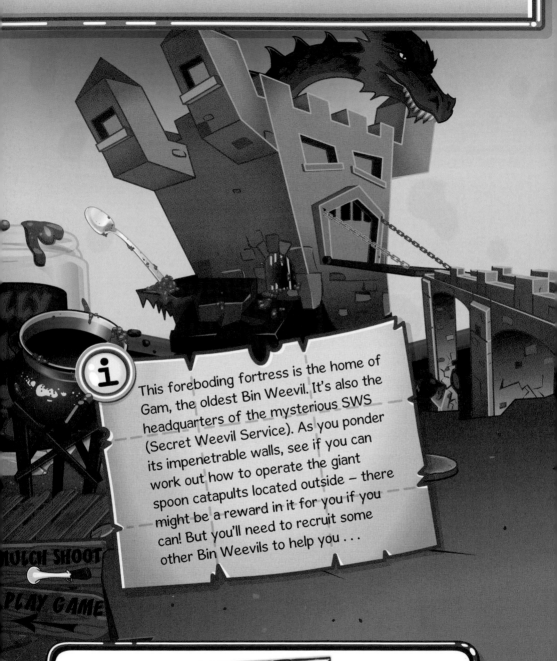

This foreboding fortress is the home of Gam, the oldest Bin Weevil. It's also the headquarters of the mysterious SWS (Secret Weevil Service). As you ponder its impenetrable walls, see if you can work out how to operate the giant spoon catapults located outside – there might be a reward in it for you if you can! But you'll need to recruit some other Bin Weevils to help you . . .

TOP SECRET

Castle Gam is full of mysteries! Clicking on a certain brick on the outside of Castle Gam might reveal one of them to you . . .

Castle Gam

SQUARES

Aim: To make more squares than your opponent.

How to play: Take it in turns with your opponent to connect two dots with a line. When you complete a square by drawing its fourth side, the square becomes yours – so make a square whenever you can! Every time you complete a square, you get another go. You can complete long chains of squares this way.

91

MEET THE BIN WEEVILS

GAM

The glory days of this old soldier are long past, but that doesn't stop him reliving his proudest moments. Give him half a chance, and he'll take half a day telling you about the swashbuckling adventures of his youth. Just make sure you shout your approval, as he's a bit hard of hearing these days. His home, Castle Gam, is as old as he is, although it only just survived one of Tink and Clott's loony schemes. Pull up a stool, and Gam will tell you all about that too. Gam's colossal pet, a gentle dragon named Colin, lives in the dungeons below the castle!

Best moment:

Becoming the chief of the SWS.

Gam & Baby Colin!

Greatest ambition: To write his action-packed autobiography.

THE SECRET WEEVIL SERVICE

TOP SECRET

Op...CRET...
...Report

Ref No. ....
DC/FI Bin Section

Special Agents T... and C...

AGENT TINK

AGENT CLOTT

Once you've gained access to Gam's castle, you will find yourself at the heart of the SWS headquarters. If you are ready to serve your fellow Bin Weevils and join the elite ranks of those who have sworn to protect the Bin, then accept the challenge and enlist in SWS missions here! Are you brave enough to take on the Weevil Extermination Bureau, the Bin's fiercest foes? The WEB are lurking nearby . . .

SWS MISSIONS

TROUBLE AT CASTLE GAM!

Your SWS mission is to save Castle Gam from being flooded with slime! Find your way through the maze to reach the control room and help Rigg fix the pipes before it's too late!

You'll have to negotiate your passage with Gam's guards, solve riddles and puzzles, and explore the dark dungeon with nothing more than a torch for light. It's definitely not for the faint-hearted Bin Weevil, but the rewards are great if you keep your wits about you.

The Entrance

The Pipe Room

The Cavern

SECRET CODE

SWS Agents, we've just received a top-secret code! Hold this page up to a mirror to reveal the code, then enter it in the Mystery Code Machine at Lab's Lab to unlock a free nest item!

AB2XWA272ðA2W2

TOP TIP
Completing SWS missions is a Bin-tastic way to earn some amazing rewards and rare items for your nest!

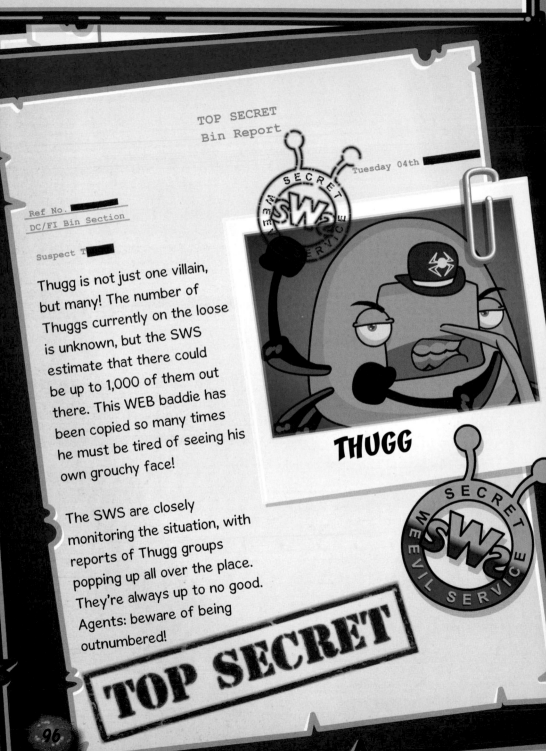

TOP SECRET
Bin Report

Tuesday 04th

Ref No. ▮▮▮▮▮
DC/FI Bin Section

Suspect T▮▮

Thugg is not just one villain, but many! The number of Thuggs currently on the loose is unknown, but the SWS estimate that there could be up to 1,000 of them out there. This WEB baddie has been copied so many times he must be tired of seeing his own grouchy face!

The SWS are closely monitoring the situation, with reports of Thugg groups popping up all over the place. They're always up to no good. Agents: beware of being outnumbered!

THUGG

SECRET
MEEVIL SERVICE

TOP SECRET

TOP SECRET

Ref No. ▩▩▩▩/▩▩

DC/FI Bin Section

Suspect W▩▩▩▩ ▩

Wednesday 24th ▩▩▩▩▩ ▩▩▩▩

This crafty little bad guy is super-fast and super-evil! He's the WEB's jack-of-all-trades: pet-napper, getaway driver, demolition expert and master thief. Some suspect that Weevil X may be the brains behind the WEB, but evidence suggests that he's carrying out the dirty work for the WEB's shadowy arch-villain.

Top priority for the SWS is to discover Weevil X's true identity. Can he possibly be brought over from the dark side? He would make a priceless double agent in the fight against the WEB.

WEEVIL X

MULCH SHOOT

Think you're a good shot? Look carefully at these balls of flying Mulch, then close your eyes and draw a cross with a pen where you think each one is. How many did you get?

LEVEL

5

A fast-paced game for the sharp-eyed Bin Weevil! Pick up your trusty shotgun and blast away at some Mulch as it hurtles through the sky. It starts off easy, but it gets a lot harder – soon the Mulch will be flying thick and fast!

WHACK A WEEVIL

TOP TIP
If you're quick enough to land a hit on sneaky Weevil X, you'll earn extra points!

The WEB are up to their old tricks again and they're tearing up Flem's beautiful lawn! Can you help knock back these creepy critters before they take over?

Use your swatter to swat the baddies as they appear from the holes. The more WEB agents you hit, the more points you'll score! But watch out, if you hit a helpful SWS agent, you'll lose points.

You can find Whack a Weevil on the grounds of Flem Manor.

99

MULCH ISLAND

For Bin Weevils who want to get away from it all, Rum's Airport is the right destination. Step up to the check-in desk, pick up your ticket (price: FREE!) and board a plane bound for the exotic Mulch Island! From desert sands to ancient ruins, there's no telling how many secrets this island holds.

Chill out in the sand, listen to the waves and grab an ice-cold snack from the Ice Cream Machine as you bask in the sunshine with all your friends on Mulch Beach! There's never a rainy day in this party spot, so if you're feeling blue there's no better place for a break.

Sandcastles and ice cream . . .
Yum, Yum, Yum!

If you're in the mood to explore, Mulch Island holds many mysteries. SWS agents have been investigating some ancient ruins around the island, and hidden messages have been discovered by those who dig . . . There's much more here than meets the eye, but it will take cleverness and puzzle-solving skills to unlock the island's secrets. So keep your eyes peeled for unusual artefacts and archaeological sites!

SECRET
WEEVIL SERVICE

TINK'S BLOCKS

Why not begin your visit with a game of Tink's Blocks!

How to play: When blocks of the same colour are touching, click on one to make them all disappear. You can click on the arrows to rotate the board ninety degrees in either direction – this will make all the blocks fall down to the bottom.

DID YOU KNOW?
You can take a shortcut to Tink's Blocks by clicking on it from your Buddy List Leaderboards instead of flying all the way to Mulch Island!

TOP TIP
Don't leave single blocks of one colour behind – you'll never be able to get rid of them!

Quote:

'Every day is an adventure!'

FLAM

Flam really wishes she was a fly – but since she hasn't yet managed to sprout a pair of wings, she's decided to become a pilot so she can still take to the skies! At the controls of her trusty biplane, Flam can often be found zooming to unknown islands and exploring strange exotic places. She never forgets to send a postcard, even if sometimes she has to make her own out of a piece of tree bark.

Best moment: Her very first flight in her own plane!

Greatest ambition: To travel into space!

Quote:
'It's all about me!'

POSH

Posh is sweet, sophisticated and always demands the best! Dosh's little sister loves everything luxurious, so it's a good thing she's part of the Bin's richest family. Posh is always first in line for the latest cool nest item or a fancy new hat, and she's always redecorating her rooms in Dosh's Palace. The only thing she loves more than shopping (and gazing at her own reflection) is her pampered Bin Pet, Lady Wawa, who never strays far from her side.

Best moment:

Adopting her Bin Pet, Lady Wawa!

Greatest ambition: To throw a mega-party and shower the entire Binscape with glitter!

TUM'S DINER

Now that you're back from your trip to the island, you're probably craving some good honest weevily nosh. Tum runs this place with the help of her unglamorous assistant Slum, but her dream is to be a TV chef. Pull up a seat, or put on an apron and lend a hand – they could always use one!

Burger
side
he Bin!

Tum's been working on some gags for her TV show, but Slum's mixed them up. Can you match the joke with the punchline?

1. What do you find on tiny beaches?
2. What's a vampire's least favourite food?
3. What did the astronaut eat his dinner from?
4. What's white and fluffy and lives in the rainforest?
5. What vegetable do you never want to find in a boat?

The answers are on page 159.

D. Microwaves!

C. Steak!

E. A meringue–utan!

A. A satellite dish!

B. A leek!

THE HAGGLE HUT

GONG'S PIPENEST

Make your way to Gong's Pipenest, where you can enter competitions to win awesome prizes, or pay a visit to Nab's Haggle Hut and sell your unwanted stuff!

Gong's Pipenest

THE HAGGLE HUT

Selling unwanted items at the Haggle Hut is a quick way to top up your Mulch reserves. But beware of Nab's tricks when you're making a deal!

Quote:

'Wanna make a deal?'

NAB

Greatest ambition:

To outwit Tink and Clott.

Strapped for Mulch? Then Nab's the Bin Weevil you want to find. He runs the Haggle Hut at Gong's Pipenest and is always ready and willing to buy your unwanted nest items and strike a 'good bargain' (good for him, of course!). He'll even let you play a game to earn a chance for a better deal. But beware! He's known for being a bit cheeky, so if you dare to take a chance, you could find yourself with considerably less to show for it! As Nab always likes to say, 'Finders keepers!'

Best moment: When he stole one of Tink and Clott's jobs.

TINK'S TREE

Tink's Tree is a magical area where Bin Weevils can cooperate to make great things happen!

By feeding flies to the tree's roots, you can help Tink's Tree to blossom and fruit.

First you'll need to climb into the canopy to activate the yellow fly nest. Use the mushroom steps and branches to get there.

Once you've found the fly nest, the flies will be buzzing around looking for something sweet.

Back on the ground, you'll have to scent your Bin Weevil with a Scent Flower to attract the flies, which will begin to circle around your Bin Weevil's head.

Move closer to the tree's feeding roots and the tree will gobble up the flies, helping the fruit to grow.

Continue to feed the tree until it finally blossoms and bears fruit! When the fruit is ripe, the tree will drop seeds that Bin Tycoons can collect.

Quick, quick! Pick up the seeds before they're gone and plant them in your garden to see what blooms.

Inside Tink's Tree you'll find another way up!

All the seeds look exactly the same, but you'll be surprised at what they might turn into . . .

Scent Flower	Step Mushroom	Tink's Tree

TYCOON ISLAND

Tycoon Island is the place to be in the Binscape! From the moment you touch down in a gold-plated helicopter, you're in for some serious fun. Stroll through the luxurious shopping plaza and shop till you drop, or chillax and put your feet up at the Smoothie Shack while enjoying a tune from the Jam Stand! Famous Bin Weevils are often seen on the helipad, making Tycoon Island a perfect haunt for a bit of celeb-spotting! It's no wonder that Bunty, the most starstruck Bin Weevil, loves to hang around here waiting for autograph opportunities!

TOP SECRET

Click on all the windows of the Tycoon Restaurant to light them up and see what happens . . .

112

TYCOON TV TOWERS

Watch cool cartoons and TV shows in the exclusive Bin Tycoon cinema at Tycoon TV Towers! Join your buddies and watch together for twice as much fun!

If you prefer a night in, invite your friends to your nest and chill out in your home cinema room, where you can enjoy a show with pals in custom-decorated luxury. Decorate your cinema room with everything from comfy cushions to snazzy speakers!

Home Cinema

THE SLIME POOL

The Slime Pool is THE place for Tycoons to hang out. Whizz down a water slide into a huge bath of slime, or chill with your buddies at the poolside with a refreshing drink while the band plays laid-back tropical grooves.

TOP TIP

To get down quickly you can also use the trampolines floating in the Slime Pool!

THE SMOOTHIE SHACK

SMOOTHIE SHACK
PLAY GAME

You can earn some extra Mulch by making smoothies for thirsty Bin Weevils in the Smoothie Shack game, or make some music of your own at the Jam Stand instead.

The price of each smoothie is the cost of all its ingredients added together. Can you work out the cost of each ingredient on its own?

 Peach on the Beach = 13 Mulch

 Lime Slime = 12 Mulch

 Groovie Smoothie = 17 Mulch

 Awesome Poursome = 14 Mulch

TYCOON PLAZA

Tycoon Plaza is home to the most exclusive (and expensive) boutiques in the Bin. If Mulch and Dosh is no object, you'll find everything you need to kit out your businesses, satisfy your passion for fashion and decorate your home cinema room. Turn right when you exit the helicopter and step into shopping paradise!

Look out for the Mulch-encrusted statue of Dosh! He's a huge inspiration to up-and-coming Tycoons and the fabulously wealthy!

121

HEM

Quote:

'Are you still wearing that, darling?'

Hem is the Bin's most talented seamstress and fashion designer, and hats are her absolute speciality! Hem is constantly pestering Scribbles to write about her latest hat designs in WEEVIL WEEKLY. If she isn't busy sketching a design for some new headwear, she's out and about modelling it! Hem believes in always looking her best, and she keeps her shop stocked with everything you need to make a real weevily fashion statement! From the sweet and stylish to the weird and wacky, Hem's got the hat for you. One minute you can sport an impressive jewelled crown, the next you could be right at home in Lab's Lab with the Lightbulb Helmet.

Best moment

Opening her Hat Shop on Tycoon Island

Greatest ambition:

To see every Bin Weevil wearing one of her creation

HEM'S HATS

Salute spring with this lavish lid!

You're sure to stand out in a crowd!

Show off like retro royalty!

MEET THE BIN WEEVILS

BUNTY

Greatest ambition:

To collect the autograph of every Bin celebrity.

Quote:
'Oh my gosh, have you heard the latest?'

Bunty is a Bin Weevil who just loves to know what's going on. If there's some gossip going round the Bin, Bunty is sure to know about it – she might well have started it! Bunty is a loyal reader of WEEVIL WEEKLY, so she can pass on all the tastiest stories to her friends. She also loves celebrities, and she's always hanging out backstage at Tycoon TV Towers, trying to get autographs. There's no such thing as a quick chat with Bunty. In fact, Hem rang her last Friday and we hear that Bunty still hasn't hung up the phone!

Best moment:
Getting her first backstage pass.

THE TYCOON SHOP

Surround yourself with epic sound!

Admire it while watching BWTV!

Get comfy, sit back and enjoy the show!

GARDEN PLOTS

EXIT

Bin Tycoons can expand their garden up to FOUR times! With so much space in which to plant, you'll soon be totally surrounded by lush trees, colourful mushrooms and beautiful blooms! Not to mention the oodles of room you'll have to display statues, scarecrows and even a full set of lawn furniture!

TOOLS

GROW MORE

Super-Deluxe Garden

Larger Garden

Deluxe Garden

SNAPPY

Quote:

'Say cheese!'

Greatest ambition:

To open a photo gallery in Flem Manor.

Snappy is the Bin's photography expert. She's got the best advice and all the best backdrops to make your Photo Studio as successful as can be! Snappy can seldom be found without a camera in hand, and she loves a mag that's packed with great photos. But we'll let you in on a little secret: Snappy is actually super-shy and hates to have her own photo taken! She prefers to be behind the lens rather than in front of it. You can find Snappy in her Photo Studio shop on Tycoon Island.

Best moment:

When her idea for the Bin Tycoon Photo Studio was introduced to the Bin.

THE PHOTO SHOP

THE PARTY SHOP

Fling's Party Shop is the place to be when you're ready to kit out your new club. From neon lights to a glittering dance floor, Fling has all you need to make your business catch everyone's weevily eye!

YOUR TYCOON PLAZA

Bin Weevils can access your Tycoon Plaza through the button on the floor in your nest, so the more people you invite to your nest, the more visitors you'll get to your plaza. Your plaza can also be found by clicking on your name in the Tycoon Directory (in the top hat in front of the Shopping Mall).

TYCOON PLAZAS

Juke Nuke	
Mylo47	
fuzzy_101	
doolie	
lucas_bonchance	
super_taffy	
Gnu	
mallony2	

01-08 of 47

List of Bin Weevil businesses

Whenever Bin Weevils enter your businesses or buy a picture from your Photo Studio, you'll earn Mulch! To see how much Mulch you've earned, collect it from the cash machine in Rigg's Multiplex.

MONSTA STOMP

You can buy new party fronts and decorate your Tycoon Plaza, just like you do your nest.

If you want to be listed in the Tycoon Directory so that other players can see your name in the top hat, remember to open your plaza each time you log in! To open your plaza, click on the red lock on the right-hand side. It'll turn to green, and voila! You're open for business!

YOUR PARTY ROOM

Create the perfect place for your friends to party all day and all night! Pick out the coolest furniture, lights, speakers, dance floor and decorations, then spin the best dance tracks to make your party the place to be! Don't forget to take out your Tycoon Camera and snap some pics of the VIPs for your magazine – all your guests will love the limelight!

Earn Mulch when other Bin Weevils spend time in your party room! You can collect this from the cash machine.

My friends love to party!

Keep fit by moving to the groove!

YOUR PHOTO STUDIO

Decorate your photo studio with exotic backdrops or seasonal props! The better your set, the more Bin Weevils will want their picture taken in your studio. Whenever your plaza is open or you invite guests to your nest, your studio will be accessible to anyone who wants a snapshot. Only you can change the backdrop, though, so keep things fresh with some fun accessories and invite everyone to be a shutterbug!

Earn **Mulch** when other Bin Weevils purchase pics from your studio! Mulch earned can be collected from the cash machine.

Bin Weevils at work!

Happy Chinese New Year!

WHICH BIN WEEVIL ARE YOU?

WHICH BIN WEEVIL ARE YOU?
STARTING AT NUMBER ONE,
ANSWER THE QUESTIONS
AND SEE WHO YOU'D
BE IN THE BIN!

1 Would you rather be rich or famous?
Revoltingly rich!
Go to 11
Fabulously famous!
Go to 8

2 Are you good with money?
I'm always trying to get my hands on more.
Go to 3
I always seem to have plenty.
Go to 10

3 You are Bunty – you're sociable and chatty, and like nothing more than a good gossip with your friends.

4 Do you love to know everything that's going on?
I just love getting all the gossip!
Go to 3
I don't usually know what day it is . . .
Go to 10

5 Do you ever lose your temper?
No, I'm always calm and reasonable.
Go to 3
Sometimes things make me mad!
Go to 10

6 Are you a hard worker?
I always give 121% (that's 110% of 110%)!
Go to 3
I'd rather someone else did the hard work.
Go to 10

7 You are Lab – you're something of a brainbox, and you always want to know more.

138

8

Caviar and silk sheets all the way, please!

Go to 1

I don't need fancy things to be happy.

Go to 5

13

You are Tink – you've always got a cunning plan, and a buddy to help you make it happen.

9

Do you like being the centre of attention?

Yes! Everyone, look at me!

Go to 2

I'm happy to take a back seat.

Go to 14

14

Do you like taking orders?

I'm happy to do what I'm told.

Go to 10

Nobody pushes me around!

Go to 12

10

You are Clott – honest and loyal, you're always happy to help your friends.

15

Are you good at remembering facts?

Yes, I store them in my 100 billion brain cells!

Go to 7

I'm always forgetting . . . erm . . . things.

Go to 13

11

Which school subject do you prefer?

Clever stuff like maths and science.

Go to 6

Active stuff like games and drama.

Go to 9

16

You are Dosh – a born leader with a taste for the finer things in life.

12

You are Rott – you speak your mind, and you're not afraid to stand up for yourself!

17

Are you good at coming up with ideas?

Yes. In fact, I've just had one now!

I'm not really an ideas person.

ALL ABOUT YOU

Favourite trophy:

Bin Weevil name:

_____

Date you joined Bin Weevils:

Date you became a Bin Tycoon:

Best moment:

Bin Pet's name:

Magazine name:

Famous Bin Weevil you'd most like to meet:

IN THE BIN

Favourite place to hang out:

Favourite Bin party:

Favourite game:

Favourite shop:

Favourite Brain Strain subject:

YOUR WEEVILY LOOKS

Draw some of the weevily looks you've sported! Changing your
look is easy – just visit the Bin Weevil Changer at Dosh's Palace!

MORE ABOUT YOU

YOUR BIN NEST

Favourite nest items:

1

2

3

4

5

Favourite plants:

1

2

3

Favourite hats:

1

2

3

Which SWS missions have you completed?

142

Toughest mission:

Favourite SWS reward:

YOUR BIN BUDDIES

Draw two of your best Bin buddies and record some of their vital stats!

Bin buddy name:

Fave place in the Bin:

Fave thing to do together:

Fave thing about this buddy:

Bin buddy name:

Fave place in the Bin:

Fave thing to do together:

Fave thing about this buddy:

BIN TASK CHECKLIST

BEGINNER

Purchase an item from the Shopping Mall ☐

Plant and harvest a seed in your garden ☐

Decorate your first nest room ☐

Win Mulch by playing a game ☐

Watch a Bin Weevils cartoon ☐

Race at Dirt Valley ☐

Stamp your BinCard ☐

Add a Bin buddy ☐

Get a Mulch-tastic ticket ☐

Invite someone to visit your nest ☐

Rate another Bin Weevil's nest ☐

Take a flight to Mulch Island ☐

Buy a photo in a Bin Tycoon Photo Studio ☐

Complete a wordsearch ☐

Reach Level 10 ☐

INTERMEDIATE

Adopt your very own Bin Pet ☐

Collect a Bin Bot ☐

Build your own Weevil Wheels track ☐

Change your Bin Weevil's look at Dosh's Palace ☐

Help grow the mushrooms at Flum's Fountain ☐

Help Tink's Tree blossom and collect a seed ☐

Complete an SWS mission ☐

Outwit Nab at the Haggle Hut ☐

Collect some XP from the cannon at Club Fling ☐

Open your own Photo Studio ☐

Finish assembling a puzzle on your BinCard ☐

Create and publish your own magazine ☐

Redeem a secret code at the Mystery Code Machine ☐

Buy a cool hat from Hem's Hat Shop ☐

Reach Level 20 ☐

EXPERT

Get on the cover of another Bin Weevil's magazine ☐

Train your Bin Pet to juggle nine balls ☐

Grab a rare seed from Tink's Tree ☐

Complete five whole BinCards ☐

Become a Track Tester at Dirt Valley ☐

Earn a trophy from the Nest Inspector ☐

Reach level 40 ☐

THE WEEVILY ZODIAC

WHAT'S YOUR WEEVILY STAR SIGN?

Did you know that your golden Birthday Egg tells you the date when your Bin Weevil was created? If you spot a golden egg in your buddy's nest, click on the egg to see when their Bin Weevil's birthday is! Check out the star signs below, find your Bin Weevil's birthday and see what it reveals about your personality . . .

Aries (Mar 21–Apr 19)

Aries Bin Weevils like to get things done, and they're always on the move. From playing multiplayer games to zooming around the racetrack at Dirt Valley, they're going somewhere and they're going there fast! Aries Bin Weevils have loads of friends, but they're hard to keep up with because they're just sooooo busy! Aries are born leaders, so you're likely to find them coordinating an effort to get the XP meters filled at Club Fling.

Taurus (Apr 20–May 20)

Stubborn but extremely patient, a Taurus Bin Weevil is willing to save for ages to accumulate enough Mulch for that ultra-luxurious nest item. A loyal and trustworthy friend, Taurus can often be found in social areas like Flum's Fountain or Castle Gam. Taurus Bin Weevils make great SWS agents, with their careful thinking and excellent puzzle-solving skills!

Gemini (May 21–Jun 20)

Gemini Bin Weevils have the 'gift of the gab', so you can be sure to find them chat-chat-chatting! They love to learn and explore, so if they're not off completing the latest mission, you might find them taking their Bin Pet for a walk to see what's what in the Binscape. Geminis love change, so the Bin Weevil Changer at Dosh's Palace is one of their favourite places to be seen.

Cancer (Jun 21–Jul 22)

Cancer Bin Weevils have great communication skills. They love making new mags and working on word puzzles in Flem Manor. Resourceful and inventive, they like to collect lots of interesting nest items and find creative ways to display them. Don't be surprised if they make it into the pages of BEST NEST magazine by impressing the Nest Inspector with their ideas.

Leo (Jul 23–Aug 22)

Leo Bin Weevils love to be the centre of attention. You can usually find them right in the middle of whatever's happening in the Binscape, eager to be the first in line to check out parties and activities. Leo Bin Weevils are all about looking their best, so you're more than likely to spot them browsing around Hem's Hat Shop for the biggest, boldest, craziest hats and crowns!

Virgo (Aug 23–Sep 22)

Organized and helpful, Virgo Bin Weevils are excellent friends. Always ready to lend a helping hand, they love to cooperate on missions or join a buddy for a round of games. Their Bin Nests are meticulously neat, and they're known for planning out their rooms to the last detail. When they're not hanging with their pals, you can find them in the Shopping Mall, checking back for that perfect item.

Libra (Sep 23–Oct 22)

Libra Bin Weevils adore everything that's beautiful and green. They love the outdoors, and tending to their Bin Garden is one of their favourite things to do – spotting a rare seed in the Garden Shop always makes their day. Libras can seem quiet and a little bit reserved when you first meet them, but if you take time to make friends with them, they'll definitely stay your loyal buddies forever!

Scorpio (Oct 23–Nov 21)

Scorpios are brave and courageous, which is why so many of them have impressed the SWS with their performance on top-secret missions. Active and excitable, you can find them performing crazy special moves at Flum's Fountain or hitting the dance floor at Club Fling. They're also keen racers, so look out for them speeding around the tracks at Dirt Valley.

Sagittarius (Nov 22–Dec 21)

Sagittarians are known for wanting more, more, more! Their quest to level up is never-ending, and they sure know how to apply themselves to the task. They live for earning XP, harvesting their garden regularly and playing all the games they can lay their weevily hands on. As a result of their hard work, their Bin Nests are absolutely spectacular, and their nest coolness is off the chart.

Capricorn (Dec 22–Jan 19)

Capricorns are playful and fun-loving. Always looking on the bright side of things, they'll surely cheer up a friend who's feeling blue. Skilled in problem-solving and strategy, they excel at games like Flip Mulch and Squares, but they're so darned nice that they might just let you win once in a while. Capricorn Bin Weevils are excellent Bin Pet owners. Their pets are well cared for and can do the craziest tricks!

Aquarius (Jan 20–Feb 18)

Aquarius Bin Weevils love to explore. You can bet they've wandered through every nook and cranny in the Binscape, and if there are hidden secrets to be uncovered, they are quickly on the case. Outgoing and friendly, Aquarians love to meet new buddies. One of their favourite pastimes is helping to unleash the Mulch catapult at Castle Gam, especially because they can chat while they're doing it!

Pisces (Feb 19–Mar 20)

Pisceans love water, and so these Bin Weevils especially love to visit Mulch Island. On the beach, they can listen to the waves lapping while they enjoy a cold ice cream. They're also really creative, so their magazines are bound to be an exciting read. Pisces Bin Weevils believe strongly in the power of luck, so they never forget to collect their daily Mulch-tastic ticket, and they enter every competition.

LET'S MAKE A DEAL

Make a deal with your parent(s) to get Bin Tycoon membership! Offer to help out a little more around the house or do some extra chores to make them happy. Don't pester them, but show them how responsible you are and they just might make you a Bin Tycoon!

Here are some ideas to start you off:

- ○ Clean up your room
- ○ Make your bed in the morning
- ○ Make breakfast for your family
- ○ Do the dusting
- ○ Do the vacuuming
- ○ Help with the laundry
- ○ Fill or empty the dishwasher
- ○ Wash the dishes

- ○ Watch your little brother/sister
- ○ Help with the shopping
- ○ Help out in the garden
- ○ Take out the rubbish
- ○ Feed or walk the family pet
- ○ Wash the car
- ○ Lay the table for dinner
- ○ Clean up the kitchen after dinner

I, _____(your name),

promise to complete the following chores and responsibilities

for _____(length of time)

to earn Bin Tycoon membership on Bin Weevils!

WHAT I WILL DO	WHEN I WILL DO IT
Lay the table for dinner	Every day at 6 p.m.

_____

Your signature

Membership is available in one-month, six-month and twelve-month instalments. Turn to page 16 to learn more about becoming a Bin Tycoon.

FABULOUS FAN ART

paul206gti

Ninja40

BINGIY465

By Smashbin 31

Wow! A new island

smashbin31

rainbow2203

lizzy3344

friends7011

wotawotal

siener525

153

HOW TO DRAW A BIN WEEVIL

1

First draw a triangle for the head, overlapping a square for the body.

Draw your lines in pencil until you're finished. If you make a mistake, you can just rub it out!

2

Now draw lines down and across the head. This will help you position the eyes and nose. The eyes are two circles, one inside the other. For the nose draw two sausage shapes. Add antennae.

3

For each arm and leg, simply draw two sausage shapes. One short and fat, one long and thin!

4

The hands are two circles and a sausage for the thumb. Draw an outline around the shapes to make the hand.

Next, draw ten squashed ovals. These are the elbows, knees and feet of your Bin Weevil.

5

To finish your Bin Weevil, simply draw over your pencil lines in the colour of your choice.

Now that you can draw this Bin Weevil, why not try designing your own?

INVITE A FRIEND

3 FRIENDS

1 FRIEND

5 FRIENDS

2 FRIENDS

Have you got some friends who might enjoy Bin Weevils? Invite your friends to join the fun, and you could transform your nest into an undersea paradise with your very own floor-to-ceiling AQUARIUM!

)SH   INVITE A FRIEND   WHAT'

Click on INVITE A FRIEND at the top of the page (you must be logged in to see it) and let all your pals know about the fun you're having in the Binscape!

6 FRIENDS

4 FRIENDS

7 FRIENDS

8 FRIENDS

9 FRIENDS

When your first friend accepts your invitation and joins Bin Weevils, you will get an Aquarium item for FREE and your friend will get 1000 extra Mulch. The more friends you invite, the more critters you can earn for your Aquarium. Fill your Aquarium with crazy creatures, fish and fun stuff and welcome new buddies to the Bin!

ANSWERS

EXCLUSIVE NEST ITEM!
Get an exclusive nest item by gathering the following info from this book to reveal a secret code! Enter your code into the Mystery Code Machine in front of Lab's Lab to claim your surprise.

1. What is the first word in the Garden Inspector's quote?
2. How many yellow squares are on the Tink's Blocks game board on page 103?
3. What is the name of Gam's pet dragon?
4. How much XP do you earn by collecting a green mushroom at Flum's Fountain?
5. What does Posh want to cover the Binscape with when she throws her party?

Put all your answers together to reveal your secret code!

1. __ __   2. __   3. __ __ __ __ __   4. __   5. __ __ __ __ __ __

Pages 68-69: FIGG'S CAFE:
CLOTT, SCRIBBLES, DOSH, FLING, NEST INSPECTOR.
Page 79: THE DAILY BRAIN STRAIN:

How many squares? **3**

How many circles? **4**

$4 \times ? = 16$ → **4**

$23 - 9 = ?$ → **14**

A.M. **04:10**

P.M. **21:25**

Japan

Page 81: SPOT THE DIFFERENCE: Did you spot the ten differences on the dance floor? They are circled in this photo.

Pages 82-83: WORD PUZZLES:

Page 107: TUM'S DINER: 1 D; 2 C; 3 A; 4 E; 5 B.

Page 117: THE SLIME POOL: Pipe A.

Page 119: THE SMOOTHIE SHACK:

6 3 5

Goodbye!

That's it from us . . .
until the next book . . .
Fall in, flip out, and see you in the Bin!

Scribbles